The adventures of otto

Go, Otto, Go!

David Milgrim

Ready-to-Read

Simon Spotlight

New York   London   Toronto   Sydney   New Delhi

SIMON SPOTLIGHT
An imprint of Simon & Schuster Children's Publishing Division
1230 Avenue of the Americas, New York, New York 10020
This Simon Spotlight edition May 2016
Copyright © 2016 by David Milgrim
All rights reserved, including the right of reproduction in whole or in part in any form.
SIMON SPOTLIGHT, READY-TO-READ, and colophon are registered trademarks of
Simon & Schuster, Inc.
For information about special discounts for bulk purchases, please contact
Simon & Schuster Special Sales at 1-866-506-1949
or business@simonandschuster.com.
Manufactured in the United States of America 0416 LAK
2 4 6 8 10 9 7 5 3 1
Library of Congress Cataloging-in-Publication Data
Names: Milgrim, David, author, illustrator.
Title: Go, Otto, go! / story and pictures by David Milgrim.
Description: First Simon Spotlight hardcover/paperback edition. | New York :
Simon Spotlight, 2016. | Series: Ready-to-read. Pre-level 1
Series: The adventures of Otto | Summary: Otto the robot builds a spaceship
to take him home.
Identifiers: LCCN 2015046177 | ISBN 9781481467230 (pbk)
ISBN 9781481467247 (hc) | ISBN 978-1-4814-6725-4 (eBook)
Subjects: | CYAC: Robots—Fiction. | Rockets (Aeronautics)—Fiction.
Classification: LCC PZ7.M5955 Go 2016 | DDC [E]—dc23 LC record available
at http://lccn.loc.gov/2015046177

See Otto.

See Otto look.

See Otto look
at his home.

See Otto work.

Work, Otto, work.

Work,

work,

work.

Look what
Otto made!

See Otto go.

See Otto go up.
Up, up, up.

Uh-oh.

See Otto go down.

Down,
down,
down.

See Otto
go here.

See Otto go there.

See Otto go . . .

. . . nowhere.

See Otto.

See Otto look.

See Otto look at
his home.

Home, sweet home!